Alice Maude Kellogg

Kellogg's Primary Recitations

100 Bright, Sparkling Selections for Thanksgiving, etc. etc.

Alice Maude Kellogg

Kellogg's Primary Recitations
100 Bright, Sparkling Selections for Thanksgiving, etc. etc.

ISBN/EAN: 9783337156138

Printed in Europe, USA, Canada, Australia, Japan

Cover: Foto ©Andreas Hilbeck / pixelio.de

More available books at **www.hansebooks.com**

KELLOGG'S

PRIMARY RECITATIONS

100 BRIGHT, SPARKLING
SELECTIONS

FOR

THANKSGIVING

WASHINGTON'S BIRTHDAY

ARBOR DAY

MAY DAY

BIRD DAY

MEMORIAL DAY

FLAG DAY

CLOSING EXERCISES

PATRIOTIC AND GENERAL OCCASIONS

NEW YORK AND CHICAGO

E. L. KELLOGG & CO.

CONTENTS.

3

CONTENTS.

Primary recitations for Christmas exercises will be found in " How to Celebrate Thanksgiving and Christmas," and a new book of " Christmas Entertainment " published by E. L. Kellogg & Co.

NOTE.

Many of the verses gathered into this little volume were written for *The Primary School.* They are distinguished from the other selections by the name of the author following directly under the title.

Thanks are due Messrs. Charles Scribner's Sons, of New York, for permission to use poems by Robert Louis Stevenson, Eugene Field, and Mrs. Julia C. R. Dorr; to Mrs. Alice W. Rollins for selections from her volume, "Little Page Fern"; Houghton, Mifflin & Co., of Boston, for Poems by Alice and Phœbe Cary; and to the publishers of *The Outlook,* of New York, *The Youth's Companion,* of Boston, and *The Independent,* of New York, for verses contributed to their pages.

Although a considerable proportion of the recitations included in this collection are suitable for special day exercises, additional ones for these occasions will be found in the different numbers of our series of "Special Day Books": "How to Celebrate Washington's Birthday," "How to Celebrate Arbor Day," "How to Celebrate Thanksgiving and Christmas," "New Year and Midwinter Exercises," "Spring and Summer School Celebrations," "Authors' Birthdays" Nos. 1 and 2, and "Christmas Entertainment."

E. L. KELLOGG & COMPANY.

Primary Recitations.

Welcome.

By Alice E. Allen.

(To be used as an opening piece on a program of primary exercises.)

Which is the sweetest of words you may hear ?
" Love " touches all hearts, and " Home " is most
    dear.
Children choose " Christmas," the weary love
    " Rest ";
But " Welcome " of all is the sweetest and best !
As violets greet Maytime, as stars greet the night,
As birds sing in chorus to welcome the light,
So, with smiles and with music, sweet greeting we
    call,
And welcome you gladly, dear friends, each and
    all !

The American Flag.

By Lena E. Faulds.

(A recitation for a flag-raising.)

Lift it high, our glorious banner;
    Let it wave upon the breeze;
Freedom's starry emblem ever,
    Lift it high o'er land and seas.

Many conflicts it has witnessed,
   Many stories it could tell
Of the brave who fought around it,
   Of the brave who 'neath it fell.

Scenes of woe and desolation,
   Scenes of joy o'er vict'ries won;
Scenes of rest and peaceful union;
   Freedom now for every one.

Lift the flag, then, high above us,
   May it wave till time shall cease,
And its record for the future
   Be of happiness and peace !

The Best Kind to Plant.

By L. F. ARMITAGE.

(To be recited by a boy on Arbor Day.)

" Yes, Jack, my boy, we'll plant a tree,
   We'll set it out with care,
And you shall choose it. Shall it be
   A walnut, spruce, or pear ? "

" Now whether birch or elm," said Jack,
   " I do not care a dime;
The kind of tree *I* want to plant
   Is one that's good to climb ! "

Our Nation's Dead.

By SUSIE M. BEST.

(A recitation.for Memorial Day.)

All over our fair land to-day
The grateful people pause and say,
" We'll gather all earth's fairest blooms
To decorate the soldiers' tombs;
For well indeed our bosoms know
The debt of gratitude we owe
To those who ventured limb and life
When war in all the land was rife."

To-day all over our fair land
The people dwell, a peace-blessed band;
From bound to bound, in home and hall,
One honored flag waves over all !
For this we bless our nation's dead,
And, as we reverently tread
Besides their graves, we place with care
Love's fadeless laurels everywhere !

The Robin's Secret.

(Give this recitation prominence in the exercises for Bird Day.)

I'm a Robin Redbreast,
  My nest is in the tree;
If you look up in yonder elm,
  My pleasant home you'll see.
We've made it very soft and nice—
  My pretty mate and I—
And all the time we worked at it
  We sang most merrily.

I have a secret I would like
 The little girls to know;
But do not tell a single boy,
 They rob the poor birds so.
Within our pretty little nest,
 Arranged with loving care,
Are five sweet speckled little eggs—
 Don't tell the boys they're there !

Winter Jewels.

(One speaker may recite these lines, and four other children, standing
in a semi-circle on the platform, accompanying her with appropriate
hand-gestures.)

A million little diamonds
 Twinkled on the trees,
And all the little maidens said,
 " A jewel, if you please ! "
But while they held their hands outstretched
 To catch the diamonds gay,
A million little sunbeams came
 And stole them all away.

The New Cook.

By Myra S. Pitkin.

(An imitation of the Irish speech must be attempted by the speaker.)

She was only two weeks from Ireland,
 Ignorant as she could be,
But she seemed good-natured and willing,
 And I thought we could agree.

So I took her into the kitchen—
　　To her everything was strange:
She didn't know how to work the pump,
　　She never had seen a range.

As it happened 'twas baking morning,
　　I thought that I could but try
To teach her how civilized beings
　　Could make huckleberry-pie.

I showed her each step of the process,
　　Doing all the work myself,
From sifting the flour to putting
　　The pies away on the shelf.

Then placing a turnover dainty
　　In the oven for our Bess,
I said, " Watch that turnover, Bridget,
　　While I go and change my dress."

I returned and found her still sitting
　　By the open oven door;
And straight upon my innocent head
　　Her wrath she began to pour.

" It's mesilf that thinks you're too mane, mum,
　　For fooling a poor girl so,
An' me jist come over from Ireland,
　　An' no other place to go.

" I've been settin' by your rid-hot stove,—
　　I didn't so much as wink,—
An' you've been gone an hour by the clock,
　　An' I'm nearly dead, I think.

" An' watchin' I've bin your wee shmall pie
    As clost, mum, as I could get,
But as shure as me name's Bridget McGinnis,
    It hasn't turned over yet ! "

Our Flag.

By M. D. STERLING.

(A recitation for Flag Day or any patriotic occasion. The speaker
holds a flag.)

You may talk about the countries
    That lie beyond the sea,
But America's the country
    That's good enough for me !

The stars and stripes ! The stars and stripes !
    Oh ! that's the flag I love. (*Waves a flag.*)
Long may we see it proudly float
    Our schools and homes above.

Our country ! It| shall ever be
    More dear to me than any other—
A home for all that are oppressed,
    Where the rich man to the poor is brother.

Red, white, and blue is our country's flag—
    The flag of the brave and free;
Red, white, and blue, wherever we go,
    Is the flag for you and me.
(*The chorus to " Columbia, the Gem of the Ocean,"
is started as the speaker leaves the platform.*)

What Would You Do?

Now if you should visit a Japanese home,
  Where there isn't a sofa or chair,
And your hostess should say, " Take a seat, sir, I
    pray,"
  Now, where would you sit ?   Tell me where.

And should they persuade you to stay there and
    dine,
  Where knives, forks, and spoons are unknown,
Do you think that you *could* eat with chopsticks of
    wood,
  And how might you pick up a bone ?

And then, should they take you a Japanese drive
  In a neat little " rickshaw " of blue,
And you found, in Japan, that your horse was a
    man,
  Now, what do you think you would do ?
    —*Mary McNeil Scott in " The Independent."*

Japanese Lullaby.

(Give the effect of a Japanese interior to the platform with screens,
mats, wall-scrolls, and fans. Fasten up a hammock and lay a large doll
in it. Select a little girl with dark eyes and hair to give the recitation.
Pin her hair high on her head and run through it two wooden knitting-
needles, and dress her in a Japanese gown with a wide sash. She swings
the hammock gently at the close of each verse.)

Sleep, little pigeon, and fold your wings,—
  Little blue pigeon with velvet eyes;
Sleep to the singing of mother-bird swinging—
  Swinging the nest where her little one lies.

Away out yonder I see a star,—
  Silvery star with a twinkling song:
To the soft dew falling I hear it calling—
  Calling and tinkling the night along.

In through the window a moonbeam comes,—
  Little gold moonbeam with misty wings;
All silently creeping, it asks " Is he sleeping—
  Sleeping and dreaming while mother sings ? "

But sleep, little pigeon, and fold your wings,—
  Little blue pigeon with mournful eyes;
Am I not swinging ?—see, I am swinging—
  Swinging the nest where my darling lies.
                                  —*Eugene Field.*

Hepaticas.

(To be recited on May-Day displaying a bunch of hepaticas.)

So cold it is, the violet ne'er ventures out or stirs;
But hepaticas come fearlessly, wrapped in their
  dainty furs.   —*Alice W. Rollins.*

The Acorn.

By Grace O. Kyle.

(The speaker holds an acorn in his hand.)

I am an acorn bold.
I live in the oak tree old.
I can fall to the earth
Which gave me birth,
Or into your hand
If beneath me you stand.

Be Kind.

By Dora Donn.

Suppose there were a telephone,
  With which to reach the ear
Of all school-children in the world,
  And surely make them hear,
This little message I would send
  To every youthful mind:
Whate'er their rank or place in life,
  To every one be kind.

Oh ! heed this message, boys and girls,
  In school, or at your play:
Be kind in everything you do,
  Be kind, in all you say,
For kindly deeds and kindly words
  Denote a noble mind,
And kindliness will make all grow
  More gentle and refined.

A Dream.

A little boy was dreaming
  Upon his mother's lap,
That the pins fell out of all the stars,
  And the stars fell into his cap.

So when his dream was over,
  What should that little boy do ?
Why, he went and looked into his cap
  And found it wasn't true,

The Reason.

By M. ELOISE JONES.

When Rachel and Jesse are both at play
Everything runs in the smoothest way;
Each dear little face is sunny and sweet,—
Watching them play is a pleasant treat.

For they never quarrel or disagree,
Nor snatch the playthings, nor come to me
With tiresome complaints that make me sorry,
As do their cousins Kate and Florrie.

I was thinking what the reason could be—
Although they're the sweetest girls I see;
So I called them up to make the case plain,
And asked them the puzzle to explain.

And Jessie looked red and shook her shy head,
While our wise little Rachel quickly said,
Smilingly droll, " I think it must be
'Cause I let Jessie, and Jessie lets me ! "

The Cat And The Bird.

Little Robin Redbreast sat upon a tree,
Up went Pussy-cat, and down went he;
Down came Pussy-cat, and away Robin ran :
Says little Robin Redbreast, " Catch me if you
    can ! "
Little Robin Redbreast hopped upon a wall,
Pussy-cat jumped after him, and almost got a fall.
Robin chirped and sang, and what did Pussy say ?
Pussy-cat said, " Mew ! " and Robin flew away,

Strength.

Who says " I will " to what is right,
" I won't " to what is wrong,
Although a tender little child,
Is truly great and strong.
—*Anna M. Pratt in " The Youth's Companion."*

Invitation.

(To be used on an Arbor Day program preceding a trip to the woods.)

Come to the forest woodland,
    The woodland sweet and wild,
Come to the forest woodland
    And be again a child.
There with the buds and flowers
    The butterflies and bees,
Wander in shadowy bowers
    Made by the whispering trees.

The Naughty Doll.

(On a table upon the platform place a Dresden vase and a drum. The
speaker points to these, while clasping a doll in her arms.)

My dolly is a dreadful care—
    Her name is Miss Amandy;
I dress her up and curl her hair,
    And feed her taffy candy.
Yet, heedless of the pleading voice
    Of her devoted mother,
She will not wed her mother's choice,
    But says she'll wed another,

I'd have her wed the china vase,
    There is no Dresden rarer;
You might go searching every place
    And never find a fairer.
He is a gentle, pinkish youth,
    Of that there's no denying;
Yet when I speak of him, forsooth !
    Amandy falls to crying.

She loves the drum,—that's very plain,—
    And scorns the vase so clever,
And, weeping, vows she will remain
    A spinister doll forever !
The protestations of the drum
    I am convinced are hollow;
When once distressing times should come,
    How soon would ruin follow !

Yet all in vain the Dresden boy
    From yonder mantel woos her;
A mania for that vulgar toy,
    The noisy drum, imbues her.
In vain I wheel her to and fro,
    And reason with her mildy;
Her waxen tears in torrents flow,
    Her sawdust heart beats wildly.

I'm sure that when I'm big and tall
    And wear long trailing dresses,
I shan't encourage beaux at all
    Till mamma acquiesces;
Our choice will be a suitor then
    As pretty as this vase is,—
Oh, how we'll hate the noisy men
    With whiskers on their faces !
                        —*Eugene Field.*

A Woodland Baby.

(A recitation for May-day exercises.)

Little Curlyhead, tucked in tight
Under a blanket snowy white,
Softly cuddled all in a heap,
Lay till springtime fast asleep.
Wake-robin called close to her ear,
" Get up, Curlyhead ! May-day is here."
So out she peeped, dear little thing,
Bonny Baby Fern, round as a ring !
—*Elizabeth H. Thomas in "The Youth's Companion."*

The Thanksgiving Feast.

By SUSIE M. BEST.

On Thanksgiving 'tis the custom
    To prepare a splendid feast,
And we all look forward to it
    From the greatest to the least !

Cook and mother in the kitchen
    Make the most delicious things,
Pumpkin-pies and lots of doughnuts,
    Round and square and cut like rings.

In the pot the big plum-pudding,
    Full of raisins and of spice,
Simmers in the boiling water
    Till it's cooked enough to slice.

Pickles, celery, and jelly—
    All of these you'll find if you
Look for them, for in the pantry
    On the shelves they're full in view.

From the heated baking-oven,
　　Every time the door is down,
Steals the warm, delicious odor
　　Of the turkey turning brown !

Oh, I tell you we are hungry
　　When at last we're called to eat,
And we all do ample justice
　　To the good things sour and sweet.

Jack Frost.

(One child asks the question in the first line ; a second child replies and
both run off the platform at the end.)

Where do you live, Jack Frost ?
　　In the wind when the trees are tossed,
　　In the ice when the river is crossed,
　　In the snow when the sheep are lost,
　　And in your little cold nose !

The Story of Peterkin Paul.

By Susie M. Best.

There was once a boy named Peterkin Paul,
Who was not very big nor yet very small.
He had plenty to eat and plenty to wear,
But Peterkin Paul was as cross as a bear !

Nothing he had pleased Peterkin Paul,
He vowed he never was happy at all;
His mates when they saw him all hurried away,
For with Peterkin Paul none wanted to play !

You see, he was snappish, was Peterkin Paul.
If the boys wanted cricket, why, *he* wanted *ball*,
And the other way round, for I tell you that he
Was just as contrary as contrary could be !

But a day came when Peterkin Paul fell quite sick,
And Death on the heals of his illness came quick,
And mighty few sorrowed, and mighty few cried,
And some even said, it was good that he died.

Now, boys, let us not be like Peterkin Paul,
Be we young boys or old boys, or short boys or
    tall;
For if we are like him there's none will deny,
Unloved we will live, and unmourned we will die !

A Summer Song.

(These verses may be distributed among four children, if too long for
one child to memorize.)

Roly-poly, honey-bee,
    Humming in the clover,
Under you the tossing leaves,
    And the blue sky over.
Why are you so busy, pray ?
    Never still a minute,
Hovering now above a flower,
    Now half buried in it !

Jaunty robin redbreast,
    Singing loud and cheerly,
From the pink-white apple-tree
    In the morning early,

Tell me, is your early song
    Just for your own pleasure,
Poured from such a tiny throat,
    Without stint or measure ?

Little yellow buttercup,
    By the wayside smiling,
Lifting up your happy face,
    With such sweet beguiling,
Why are you so gayly clad—
    Cloth of gold your raiment ?
Do the sunshine and the dew
    Look to you for payment ?

Roses in the garden-beds,
    Lilies cool and saintly,
Darling blue-eyed violets,
    Pansies, hooded quaintly,
Sweet-peas that, like butterflies,
    Dance the bright skies under,
Bloom ye for your own delight,
    Or for ours, I wonder ?
                    —*Julia C. R. Dorr.*

The Wind.

The wind one morning sprang up from sleep,
Saying, " Now for a frolic, now for a leap !
Now for a madcap galloping chase !
I'll make a commotion in every place."

The Hickory Nut.

By GRACE O. KYLE.

I am a hickory-nut,
And a figure forlorn I cut,
For my overcoat is lost !
'Twas taken by Jack Frost,
When I came dancing down—
You see my pointed crown.

School Greeting.

By G. SCOTT.

(A recitation for the closing of school.)

I greet you now, my schoolmates dear,
With best of wishes and loving cheer;
With peace and love within my heart,
I bid you share my joy to part.

Our holidays have come at last,—
I hope they will not go too fast,
But that each day will bring you joy
And happiness without alloy.

Now that our study-time is past,
We'll run, and play, and grow so fast,
That when our school begins once more
We'll study better than before.

When playing mid the summer flowers,
We'll not forget our schoolday hours;
I hope to meet you, one and all,
When school commences in the fall.

The Swallow.

(These lines may be recited by one of the very youngest pupils upon Bird
Day or Arbor Day.)

The swallow is come !
The swallow is come !
Oh, fair are the seasons and light
Are the days that she brings,
With her dusky wings,
And her bosom so snowy and white !

Putting the World to Bed.

(Before reciting this little winter poem, the speaker should give the title
distinctly.)

The little Snow-people are hurrying down
From their home in the clouds overhead.
They are working as hard as ever they can,
Putting the world to bed.

Every tree in a soft fleecy nightgown they clothe,
Each post has its nightcap of white,
And o'er the cold ground a thick cover they spread
Before they say good-night.

And so they come eagerly sliding down
With a swift and silent tread,
Always as busy as busy can be,
Putting the world to bed.
—*Esther W. Buxton in " The Outlook."*

A Ballad of the War.

By F. H. STAUFFER.

Two little chaps with paper caps,
  Flags flying and drum beating
A charge across the meadow made
  Where flocks of geese were eating.

The geese at this set up a hiss,
  The soldier chaps sought cover,
Quite out of breath and sadly scared,—
  The cruel war was over !

Violets in Spring.

(The first two lines may be asked by one child, the rest given in response
by a second child holding a basket of violets.)

O wind, where have you been,
  That you blow so sweet ?
Among the violets
  Which blossom at your feet.

The honeysuckle waits
  For summer and for heat;
But violets in the chilly spring
  Make the turf so sweet.
                        —*Christina Rossetti.*

The Price of Greatness.

By CARRIE VAN GILDER.

(As the last line is spoken a slate is held up for inspection.)

They say that Washington's copy-books
  Were kept so neat and clean
That his mother always preserved them.
  And now they may be seen

At his old home at Mount Vernon.
  Oh, dear ! if it takes that to be great
I fear I shall fall a long way behind;
  Just see this untidy slate !

Falling Snow.

(Accompany this recitation with finger exercise.)

See the pretty snowflakes
  Falling from the sky;
On the wall and house-tops
  Soft and thick they lie.

On the window-ledges,
  On the branches bare,
Now how fast they gather,
  Filling all the air.

Look into the garden
  Where the grass was green,
Covered by the snowflakes,
  Not a blade is seen.

Now the bare black bushes
  All look soft and white,
Every twig is laden,—
  What a pretty sight !

Going a-Nutting.

By JENNIE D. MOORE.

(A recitation for October or November.)

Going a-nutting,
  Oh, what fun !
None shall escape us,
  No, not one.

Going a-nutting
  The wind blows free,
And down come the nuts
  From the great, tall tree.

We'll fill our pockets,
  Yes, every one.
In the woods a-nutting,
  Oh, what fun !

We'll take them home,
  And eat them there,
Each boy can have
  A good big share.

The woods are yellow
  And sere and brown,
In the dry, dead leaves
  The nuts drop down.

Going a-nutting,
  What rare delight !
When the wind blows free
  And the sun shines bright.

A Joke.

The man in the wilderness asked me
How many strawberries grew in the sea ?
I answered him, as I thought good,
As many red herrings as grew in the wood.

Put it Off.

By Susie M. Best.

Put it off till to-morrow, that bad, bitter thought;
Don't think it to-day, for sad ruin is wrought,
Often and often, by nursing to-day
The thoughts that to-morrow we'd banish away.

Put it off till to-morrow, that hot angry speech;
Don't say it to-day; if you do it may reach
And stab, as a venom-tipped arrow might do,
Some heart that has only fond feelings for you.

Put it off till to-morrow, that cold, cruel deed;
Don't do it to-day, for some one may need
More sadly, perhaps, than you ever can know,
The tenderest kindness that you can bestow.

Put them off till to-morrow, those things that are
    mean;
Don't do them to-day, let a night intervene,
In the calm of reflection resentment will cease,
And your bosom will harbor but white-winged
    peace.

The Daisy.

By C. Phillips.

(Dress a little girl in a dark-green muslin gown with a close cap of green
tissue-paper, long white petals turning back from the face, with a fringe
of yellow inside.)

I'm only a little daisy,
    A flower of low degree,
Just peeping above the grasses
    On hillside and on lea.

I'm only a golden circlet,
　With petals as white as snow,
A-nodding my head to the violet
　So deep in the grass below.

I'm only a little wild-flower,
　But cultured by hand divine;
I care not for another power,
　The blessings of Heaven are mine.

Bed in Summer.

In winter I get up at night
And dress by yellow candle-light.
In summer quite the other way,
I have to go to bed by day.

I have to go to bed and see
The birds still hopping on the tree,
Or hear the grown-up people's feet
Still going past me in the street.

And does it not seem hard to you,
When all the sky is clear and blue,
And I should love so much to play,
To have to go to bed by day ?
　　　　　　—*Robert Louis Stevenson.*

The Owl.

The little brown owl sits up in the tree,
And if you look well his big eyes you may see.
He says *Whit-a-whoo* when the night grows dark,
And he hears the dog howl and the little fox bark.

April.

By WILLIAM Z. GLADWIN.

A smile and a tear,
In the spring of the year,
A smile for the summer that's coming;
With bird-thrills and flowers,
And long sunny hours,
And music of wings softly humming.

A smile and a tear
In the spring of the year,
A tear for the winter that's going;
With dull-colored sky,
And snowflakes that fly,
And blasts from the northland blowing.

What the Birds Say.

(A recitation for Bird Day.)

Do you ask what the birds say ?   The sparrow, the
    dove,
The linnet, and thrush say, " I love and I love ! "
In the winter they're silent, the wind is so strong;
What it says I don't know, but it sings a loud song.
But green leaves, and blossoms, and sunny, warm
    weather,
And singing and loving all come back together;
But the lark is so brimful of gladness and love,
The green fields below him, the blue sky above,
That he sings, and he sings, and forever sings he,
" I love my Love, and my Love loves me ! "
                    —*Samuel Taylor Coleridge.*

Winter.

By Susie M. Best.

It is winter now, for sure and certain.
See, on the window, like a curtain,
Old Jack Frost has stamped with ease
Beautiful web-like traceries.

Hill and hollow and dale and mountain,
Flowing river and gushing fountain,
Every one he has pictured there,
Like an artist, on the glassy square.

It is winter now, and the sad sun tires,
He hides in the south his tropic fires;
Out of the clouds the soft snows fall.
And cover the world like a spotless pall.

It is winter now, and the winds are bitter;
From the eaves and the walls icicles glitter,
And the leafless trees like grim ghosts stand,
Gaunt and bare in the blighted land.

Wonderland.

Wonderland is here and there;
Wonderland is everywhere;
Fly not then to east or west.
On some far, uncertain quest.

Seek not India nor Japan,
Nor the city Ispahan,
Where to-day the shadows brood
Over lonely Zendarood,

Somewhere smileth far Cathay
Through the long resplendant day;
Somewhere, moored in purple seas,
Sleep the fair Hesperides.

Somewhere, in vague realms remote
Over which strange banners float,
Lies, all bathed in silver gleams,
The dear Wonderland of dreams.

Yet no need to sail in ships
Where the blue sea dips and dips,
Nor on wings of cloud to fly
Where the haunts of faery lie.

For by miracle of morn
Each successive day is born;
And wherever shines the sun,
There enchanted rivers run !

Would you go to Wonderland ?
Lo ! it lieth close at hand;
Wonderland is wheresoe'er
Eyes can see and ears can hear !
                        —*Julia C. R. Dorr.*

Flowers For Memorial Day.

By C. PHILLIPS.

(Recitation to precede the decoration of soldiers' graves.)

We love the flowers, the little flowers
    So beautiful and bright;
They come to cheer our dreary hours,
    They come for our delight.

We love their rich and varied hues,
    Their forms and perfumes sweet;
We love to think 'tis God who strews
    These blessings at our feet.

They're tokens of unfailing love,
    Sweet harbingers of bliss:
They point to fairer realms above,
    E'en while they brighten this.

Then let us gently lift them up,
    Nor bruise the fragile stem,
Nor crush the tiny pearly cup
    Wherein the dew-drops blend.

But bear them to yon hill and dell,
    Where sleep the honored brave,
The heroes who in battle fell
    Our own dear land to save.

There gratefully and tenderly
    We'll place above each head
The fairest of our floral gifts,
    A tribute to our dead.

And with these simple offerings
    Let humble prayers ascend,
That war no more shall blight our **land,**
    No more shall slay a friend.

The Ballad of the Rubber-plant and the Palm.

(The quaint humor of these verses must be appreciated by the speaker
to carry it successfully to the audience.)

A Rubber-plant and a small Palm stood
　　Upon a marble floor.
From either side the fireplace
　　They scanned each other o'er.

"What do you rub?" the small Palm asked
　　His statelier neighbor tall.
"Alas!" the Rubber-plant replied,
　　"I cannot rub at all.

"If I had hands like yours," he said,
　　As wistfully he eyed
His smaller neighbor's pretty palms
　　With fingers opened wide,

"Then I could rub!"—"And yet," replied
　　The little Palm, "you see,
Though I have hands, I cannot rub,
　　And that's the rub with me.

"I wonder why it's always so:
　　That something we have got
Seems never quite complete to be
　　Without what we have not.

"I've often longed to rub my hands
　　With glee, here in my tub;
And you, no doubt, have often wished
　　You had some hands to rub.

" Now, if you were I, or I were you,—
　　No, that's not right, I see,—
But if you *and* I were you *or* I,
　　What a fine plant we should be ! "

Still, they did as all good plants should—
　　Kept green all winter long :
So no one ever knew or guessed
　　That anything was wrong.
　　　　　　　　　　—Alice W. Rollins.

The Boys We Need.

Here's to the boy who's not afraid
　　To do his share of work;
Who never is by toil dismayed,
　　And never tries to shirk.

The boy whose heart is brave to meet
　　All lions in the way:
Who's not discouraged by defeat,
　　But tries another day.

The boy who always means to do
　　The very best he can;
Who always keeps the right in view,
　　And aims to be a man.

Such boys as those will grow to be
　　The men whose hands will guide
The future of our land; and we
　　Shall speak their names with pride.

All honor to the boy who is
  A man of heart, I say;
Whose legend on his shield is this,
  " Right always wins the day."

A Kind Little Girl.

By Eva Lovett.

Last night I heard the froggies croak,
  They must be dreadful hoarse,
Their throats must hurt 'em awfully,
  Just like mine did, of course.

When I was hoarse they gave me lots
  Of sirup in a spoon;
If those poor froggies had it, too,
  I know they'd get well soon.

So—don't you tell—when nursie's gone,
  I'll climb up to the shelf,
An' get the bottle an' the spoon,
  An' give 'em some myself !

Would You Believe It?

(Two children may speak these lines, each in turn giving a verse.)

First Child :
  A morning-glory on our wall,
    With round and rosy face,
  That smiled alike on one and all,
    And lighted up the place,—
  One rainy day that flower queer
    Shut up its cheerful eye.

It looked so dull and strange, oh dear !
    It really made me sigh.
Would you believe a flower so gay
Could look so sad that rainy day ?

Second Child :
    A little maid within our walls,
        That makes our life's delight,
    Her smile like sunshine on us falls,
        When her sweet face is bright,—
    One rainy day that child of ours
        Put on a doleful pout.
    She frowned all day because the shower
        Kept her from playing out.
    Would you believe a maid so gay
    Could look so sad that rainy day ?
    —*Mary Chase Thurlow in " The Outlook."*

Little Bird Blue.

(A recitation for Bird Day or Arbor Day.)

Little Bird Blue, come sing us your song;
The cold winter weather has lasted so long,
We're tired of skates, and we're tired of sleds,
We're tired of snow-banks as high as our heads;
        Now we're watching for you,
        Little Bird Blue.

Soon as you sing, then the springtime will come,
The robins will call and the honey-bees hum,
And the dear little pussies, so cunning and gray,
Will sit in the willow-trees over the way;
        So hurry, please do,
        Little Bird Blue !

We're longing to hunt in the woods, for we know
Just where the spring-beauties and liverwort grow;
We're sure they will peep when they hear your
    first song,
But why are you keeping us waiting so long.
        All waiting for you,
        Little Bird Blue ?
—*Elizabeth H. Thomas in "The Youth's Companion."*

Our Native Land.

(A patriotic thought to be recited by the youngest pupil on Washington's
Birthday.

By C. PHILLIPS.

Other countries, far and near,
Other people hold most dear;
Other countries ne'er can be
Half so dear to you and me
As our own, our native land.
By it firmly let us stand.

The Months.

January brings the snow,
Makes our feet and fingers glow.

February brings the rain,
Thaws the frozen lake again.

March brings breezes sharp and chill,
Shakes the dancing daffodil.

April brings the primrose sweet,
Scatters daises at our feet.

May brings flocks of pretty lambs,
Sporting round their fleecy dams.

June brings tulips, lilies, roses,
Fills the children's hands with posies.

Hot July brings thunder-showers,
Apricots and gillyflowers.

August brings the sheaves of corn,
Then the harvest home is borne.

Warm September brings the fruit,
Sportsmen then begin to shoot.

Brown October brings the pheasant;
Then to gather nuts is pleasant.

Dull November brings the blast—
Hark ! the leaves are whirling fast.

Cold December brings the sleet,
Blazing fire, and Christmas treat.
                    —*Sara Coleridge.*

A Winter Song.

By A. L. P.

Away high up in a chestnut-tree
  A tiny baby is sleeping to-night,
With not a thought of the wind's cold breath,
  Or of summer days so warm and bright.

A dainty cradle the baby has,
  Cozy and soft and all of brown;
And baby is wrapped in blankets warm,
  Made of the finest, whitest down.

" Who is this baby sweet ? You ask,
  " And where can the baby's mother be ? "
A little brown bud is the baby dear,
  And the mother, I think, is the chestnut-tree.

The Snowflakes.

Softly down from the cold, gray sky,
On the withering air they flit and fly;
Resting anywhere; there they lie,—
     The feathery flowers !
Borne on the breath of the wintry day,
Leaves and flowers and gems are they,
Fresh and fair as the gay array
     Of the sunlit hours.

The Little Boy and the Sheep.

Lazy sheep, pray tell me why
In the pleasant fields you lie,
Eating grass and daises white
From the morning till the night ?
Everything can something do, ,
But what kind of use are you ?

Nay, my little master, nay,
Do not serve me so, I pray;

Don't you see the wool that grows
On my back to make your clothes ?
Cold, ah, very cold you'd be
If you had not wool from me.

True, it seems a pleasant thing
Nipping daisies in the spring;
But what chilly nights I pass
On the cold and dewy grass,
Or pick my scanty dinner where
All the ground is brown and bare !

Then the farmer comes at last,
When the merry spring is past,
Cuts my woolly fleece away
For your coat in wintry day.
Little master, this is why
In the pleasant fields I lie.

—Ann Taylor.

To My Dolly.

By JENNIE D. MOORE.

(A little girl holds a doll in her arms in such a position that the eyes will close when she puts it to sleep. When singing the lullaby she swings dolly to and fro gently.)

O dolly with the flaxen hair,
Pretty dolly, sweet and fair,
　　How I love you !

Dolly with the cheeks of pink,
You are beautiful, I think,
　　And I love you.

Shut your eyes now, dolly. Lie
In my arms. A lullaby
   I will sing you.

May some fairy guard your sleep,
Slumber sweet and slumber deep
   May it bring you.

(*Sings*. Air, chorus of "Rock a-bye-Baby.")

Hush-a-by dolly, hush-a-by, dear,
Close your blue eyes, you need have no fear,
Sleep on sweetly, while I am nigh,
Dolly, to guard you, hush-a-by.
Hush-a-by, hush-a-by, dolly so dear,
Hush-a-by, hush-a-by, while I am near,
Up and down, up and down, now low, now high,
Sleep on so soundly, hush-a-by-by.

Dandelions.

By E. L. BENEDICT.

(A recitation for May Day exercises.)

There surely is a gold mine somewhere,
   Down beneath the grass;
For dandelions are popping up
   In every place you pass.

But if you want to gather some,
   You'd better not delay,
For the gold will turn to silver soon,
   And all will blow away.

Nonsense Verses.

What would you see if I took you up
  To my little nest in the air ?
You would see the sky like a clear, blue cup
  Turned upside downwards there.

What would you do if I took you there
  To my little nest in the tree ?
My child with cries would trouble the air,
  To get what she could but see.

What would you get in the top of the tree
  For all your crying and grief ?
Not a star would your clutch of all you see—
  You could only gather a leaf.

But when you had lost your greedy grief,
  Content to see from afar,
You would find in your heart a withering leaf,
  In your heart a shining star.
                    —*George MacDonald.*

Character.

Daily deed and daily thought,
Slowly into habit wrought,
Raise that temple, base or fair,
Which men call our character.
Build it nobly, build it well :
In that temple God may dwell !
                    —*Edward W. Benson.*

Wild Carrot.

(The pupil in reciting exhibits a stalk of the wild carrot.)

Of all Queen Summer's ladies, she
    Has daintiest parasol;
You could not buy in Paris
    One prettier for a doll.
A dozen little silken ribs
    Hold everything in place,
Covered, as for a princess,
    With loveliest white lace.

            —*Alice W. Rollins.*

Pussy Willow.

By Carrie T. Smith.

(An Arbor Day recitation.)

Little pussy-willow, hanging on the tree,
Knew that pleasant spring had come,
And wished the sun to see.

Little pussy-willow growing, oh ! so fast,
Found her seamless overcoat
Too small for her at last.

Faster and faster grew pussy, alack !
Till she split her winter overcoat
Right up the back.

Then she put on a dress of silver-gray fur,
And it almost seemed
As if she must purr.

A little later, and lo and behold !
She is covered with pollen
Like shining gold.

And dear little stamens, so slender and white,
Hold their pollen-tops up
To catch the sunlight.

And inside her dress, so tiny and shy,
Are dear little seeds
All ready to fly.

But pussies must go, for the leaves will be here;
Next March is the time
When they reappear.

The Apple.

By GRACE O. KYLE.

(The child holds an apple as she recites.)

I am an apple red,
In the orchard I was bred.
You can eat me if you wish,
Or cook me in a dish,
Or give me to a friend
Who calls an hour to spend.

Good-bye, Little Flowers.

(For autumn exercises.)

Hark ! through the pine boughs
    Cold wails the blast.
Birds south are flying,
Summer is dying,
    Flower-time is past.

Cold are November skies,
　　Sunless and drear,
Goldenrod, eyelids close;
Aster, tuck in your toes;
　　Winter is here.

" Good-by, little flowers ! "
　　The icy winds sing;
Snow, blanket them over;
Sleep well, little clover,
　　Sleep till the spring.

Two Little Girls I Know.

(This recitation must be given expressively, with significant gestures.)

I know a little girl
　　(You ?　Oh no !)
Who, when she's asked to go to bed,
　　Does just so :
She brings a dozen wrinkles out,
　　And takes the dimples in;
She puckers up her pretty lips
　　And then she does begin :
"Oh dear me ! I don't see why
All the others sit up late,
　　And why can't I ? "

Another little girl I know,
　　With curly pate,
Who says, " When I'm a great big girl,
　　I'll sit up late.
But mamma says 'twill make me grow
　　To be an early bird."

So she and dolly trot away
　　Without another word.
Oh, the sunny smile and the eye so blue,
And—why, yes, now I think of it,
　　She looks like you !
　　　　　　　—*" The Youth's Companion."*

Which General ?

(For Washington's Birthday or any patriotic exercises.)

Sometimes mamma calls me " general ";
　　I wish I knew which one;
But I always try to tell the truth,
　　So I *hope* it's Washington.

But when I tell my papa that,
　　He laughs loud as he can,
And says if she calls me " general "
　　She must mean Sheridan;

Because whenever she wants me,
　　And I am out at play,
I nearly always seem to be
　　'Bout " twenty miles away."
—*Kate W. Hamilton in " The Youth's Companion."*

The Little Bird.

(A very small boy may say these words and follow the description in the
first line with three jumps on one foot.)

Once I saw a little bird come hop, hop, hop.
So I cried, " Little bird, will you stop, stop, stop ?"
And was going to the window to say " How do
　　you do ? "
But he shook his little tail and far away he flew.

The Other Tree.

By CARRIE VAN GILDER.

(For Washington's Birthday.)

Washington was one forefather.
  Who were the other three ?
Didn't any of them have birthdays ?
  I hope they had, for you see :
We never could have too many good times,
  As we do on Washington day.
Don't the history tell us, mamma,
The other three birthdays ?

Butterflies.

Butterflies are pretty things,
  Prettier than you or I.
See the color on his wings.
  Who would hurt a butterfly ?

Not to hurt a living thing
  Let all little children try.
See ! again he's on the wing.
  Good-by, pretty butterfly.

If I Had a Hatchet.

By C. PHILLIPS.

(These lines a primary girl may recite on Washington's Birthday.
When she finishes the teacher presents her with a tiny hatchet tied with a
ribbon.)

If only I had a nice little hatchet
  Just cut from the sandal-wood,
I'd deck it with gold and a ribbon to match it
  Most beautiful, bright, and good.

Then right in the corner, on my own little bracket,
  Thus neatly adorned it should stand,
Reminding us all of the boy with the hatchet
  Who grew up to rescue our land.

Remembrance.

(To be recited on Memorial Day.)

By LILLIE V. MICKEL.

A little blue violet looked up to the sky,
And nodded and smiled—I asked her why.
" O little blossom, what would you say ?
Why do you nod so glad and gay ? "
" I am telling of soldiers brave and true;
Come close, and I'll whisper it all to you."

A little brown wren with eyes so bright,
Was warbling a song at morning light.
" O little bird, what is it you say,
What are you singing all the day ? "
" Oh, the soldiers did so brave a thing,
And that is why I love to sing."

If some little child you chance to meet,
Who does not know why this day we greet,
" O little child," you all would say,
" We'll tell you why we keep this day;
We give to the soldiers love and praise
Who gave us their lives in other days."

Our Country.

(For a boy to speak at any patriotic exercises.)

Our country stands
With outstretched hands
   Appealing to her boys.
From them must flow
Her weal, her woe,
   Her anguish or her joys.

A ship she rides
O'er human tides
   Which rise and sink anon;
Each rolling wave
May prove her grave.
   O bear her nobly on.

The friends of right
With armor bright
   A valiant, truthful band,
Through God our aid
May yet be made
   A blessing to our land.

Helping Mamma.

By JENNIE D. MOORE.

(Recitation for a little girl.)

I'm only just a little girl,
   Yet I can useful be,
There's very much that can be done
   By little folks like me.

I run the errands for mamma,
   She says I do *so* well,
I always pay attention to
   What she may have to tell.

I play with baby; keep her still
   Then take her for a ride,
That helps I'm sure, and then I do,
   Oh, *lots* of things beside.

If we will try—I know we can—
   Of some good use to be,
There's very much that can be done,
   By little folks like me.

Pollywogs.

Wiggle, waggle, how they go,
   Through the sunny waters,
Swimming high and swimming low,
   Froggie's sons and daughters.

What a wondrous little tail
   Each black polly carries,
Helm and oar at once, and sail,
   For wind it never tarries.

When the sun goes in they sink
   To their muddy pillow,
There they lie, and eat and drink
   Of soft mud their fill, oh !

Wiggle, waggle, how they go !
   Knowing nothing better,
Yet they some time will outgrow
   Each his dusky fetter.

There are *other* folk, to-day,
  Who, with slight endeavor,
Give it up, and only stay
  Pollywogs forever.

              —*Augusta Moore.*

Daffy-down-dilly.

(A dainty costume of green and yellow may be prepared for the tiniest primary child to appear in on Arbor Day reciting these familiar lines.)

Daffy-down-dilly has come up to town,
In a yellow petticoat and a green gown.

A Zealous Patriot.

By Susie M. Best.

(A boy's recitation for Washington's Birthday.)

If there was a war I'd get my gun
And I'd be like General Washington;
I'd sling it over my shoulder—so—
And forth to the contest I would go.

I'd ride on a stately snow-white horse
In the very thick of the fight, of course;
I'd keep the hearts of my soldiers true,
For that is the way he used to do.

If there was a war I'd try to be
A brave defender of liberty,
I'd think of the way that Washington
Fought and conquered in days long done.

I'd be so full of a patriot's zeal
The hardships of war I would not feel;
If I died in battle, my wounds should show
I fell on the field fronting the foe.

But oh ! to be good from day to day
Is a harder task than to lead the fray;
Yet I'll do my examples and fetch the wood,
For heroes begin by being good !

The Corn.

By GRACE O. KYLE.

I am an ear of corn.
A grain was planted one morn,
It grew up tall and green;
The handsomest ever seen.
Soon it had many an ear,
But not one made to hear.
They ripened toward the fall
And the farmer plucked them all.

Kind Hearts.

Kind hearts are the gardens,
  Kind thoughts are the roots;
Kind words are the flowers,
  Kind deeds are the fruits.

Take care of your garden
  And keep out the weeds.
Fill, fill it with sunshine,
  Kind words and kind deeds.

Milkweed.

Now is the time for yachting, and the milkweed
    sets afloat,
On the blue air flecked with flower-foam, its brown
    and tiny boat.
It sets its white and silken sails, when, presto ! on
    the wind
The pretty sails float off themselves and leave the
    boat behind.

But they take with them an anchor, a brown and
    tiny seed;
And when they light they find themselves anchored
    like the weed.
The brown seed grows and grows, and with an-
    other summer's gales
New boats float lightly on the air, laden with silken
    sails.

                   —*Alice W. Rollins.*

The Small Boy and His String.

(He holds up a string as he speaks.)

What can a small boy do with a string ?
Well, I should guess about everything:

Make a cat's cradle; tie up a knot
In every place he oughtn't and ought;

Send his kite flying up in the air;
Sail his boat on the pond over there;

Make a stone-sling, and a red top spin;
Catch a small fish with the aid of a pin—

These are a few things, not nearly all;
So, under his knife, marbles, popgun, and ball,

In a boy's pocket the bottommost thing
Is always a piece of good stout string.

Six Little Sparrows.

By Amy Kahm.

Six little sparrows were flying around,
In front of my window, right near the ground.

They were chasing a bee from its nice little hive;
The bee stung one, and so there were five.

Five little sparrows were flying near the shore;
A wave came and swallowed one, and so there were
    four.

Four little sparrows trying to get free;
A net caught one, and so there were three.

Three little sparrows playing peek-aboo;
One got lost, and then there were two.

Two little sparrows were playing with a gun;
One went and shot himself, and so there was one.

One little sparrow fretting all alone,
He died too, and so there were none.

Which is Your Way?

If anything unkind you hear
About some one you know, my dear,
Do not, I pray you, it repeat
When you that some one chance to meet;
For such news has a leaden way
Of clouding o'er a sunny day.
But if you something pleasant hear
About some one you know, my dear,
Make haste—to make great haste were well—
To her or him the same to tell;
For such news has a golden way
Of lighting up a cloudy day.

When I Am Big.

(A little boy's speech to be given with a pompous manner.)

When I am big I mean to buy
    A dozen platters of pumkin pie,
A barrel of nuts, to have 'em handy,
    And fifty pounds of sugar-candy.

When I am big, I mean to wear
    A long-tailed coat, and crop my hair;
I'll buy a paper, and read the news,
    And sit up late whenever I choose.

Summer Time.

By Susie M. Best.

Oh, summer, summer, summer's here,
　　With suns and showers,
With birds and bees and full-leaved trees,
　　And gayly colored flowers.

Oh, summer, summer, summer's here,
　· Sweet breezes blowing;
In pastures green (their own demesne),
　　We hear the cattle lowing.

Oh, summer, summer, summer's here,
　　And earth rejoices;
She sings the praise of lovely days
　　With all her myriad voices.

A Candy-Pull.

Two little maids had a candy-pull,
　　Once, on a winter's day;
" The very best time that ever was,
　　And the sweetest, too ! " laughed May.

But mamma frowned, with her comb in hand:
　　" There is candy everywhere;
And as if 'tweren't scattered quite enough,
　　Here is some in Gracie's hair ! "

And Gracie's eyes with tears were blind,
　　As she clung to mamma's knee;
" I fink that this is the very worst kind
　　Of a candy-pull ! " sobbed she.

Being A Man.

(The words in italics should be given with emphasis, and each line spoken
with deliberation.)

I can tell you how to be a man—
    This is the way to begin:
Stop saying, " *I can't*," and say " *I can*,"—
March up to your work with a good stiff chin—
    That is the way to begin.

If you mean to be a man, you know
    You must do the best you can.
When the tempter comes, you must speak up,
    " *No !* "
He'll take to his heels if you talk to him so;
I've tried it myself, and that's how I know,
    For *I'm* going to be a man !

Yes, no more whining nor tears for me:
    I've left them out of my plan:
No falsehood, no words profane or low;
I turn my back on all *that*, you know,
When I start to be a *man*.

March.

By E. L. BENEDICT.

Here he comes a-roaring—old mad March !
Stirring up a panic in the branches of the larch.
All the little floury flakes he shakes about and sifts,
Until they fall affrighted into curved and scalloped
    drifts.

Shining hills and valleys out of frozen mist he
    makes,
And snowy mounds that make you think of jolly
    frosted cakes.

Working for Our Flag.

By F. URSULA PAYNE.

(A recitation for Flag Day.)

We're working for our flag each day,
    Though we are very small,
And you will hear some big folks say
    We cannot work at all.

We're working for our flag each day,
    And each good deed we do
Is like a little budding flower
    Around our flag so true.

We're working for our flag each day,
    Our bright and starry flag;
We'll spend our lives without a fear,
    In working for our flag.

Golden Keys.

A bunch of golden keys is mine,
To make each day with gladness shine.
" Good-morning," that's the golden key
That unlocks every day for me.
When evening comes, " Good-night," I say,
And close the door of each glad day.
When at the table, " If you please "
I take from off my bunch of keys.

When friends do anything to me,
I use the little " Thank you " key.
" Excuse me," " Beg your pardon," too,
When by mistake some harm I do;
Or, if unkindly harm I've given,
With " Forgive me " I shall be forgiven.
On a golden ring these keys I'll bind;
This is its motto, " Be ye kind."
I'll often use each golden key,
And then a child polite I'll be.

My Little Neighbor.

By AGNES M. MANNING.

(A recitation for Bird Day.)

A bird sits singing in our tree;
This is the song she sings to me:
" Oh, don't you touch my little nest !
But leave my birdies there at rest."

Every morn when I awake,
Some crumbs of bread to her I take;
Every night she waits to see
That I'm in bed and sings to me.

The National Colors.

(To be spoken on Flag Day or any patriotic occasion.)

The red has been dyed with the blood of the brave,
Who perished while fighting a nation to save;
The white is the snow, as new-fallen it lies;
The union, a square of the star-lighted skies.
                                    —W. I. Davis.

An April Day.

By Anna M. Pratt.

On an April day,
When things fell out in an April way,
The heavens were suddenly overcast,
The sky grew black and the rain fell fast;
Swiftly the tears began to rise
  In Marjorie's eyes.

On an April day,
When her sport was lost by an hour's delay,
I watched a dear child struggle the while;
She conquered her tears with a pleasant smile,
Till I saw the sunshine I missed from the skies
  In Marjorie's eyes.

On an April day,
When it suddenly cleared in an April way,
The sun shone out and the rainbow grew;
We gazed with delight, but for me there were two,
For her smile through her tears were the rainbow's
 guise
  In Marjorie's eyes.

The Way.

Good morrow, fair maid, with lashes brown.
Can you tell me the way to Womanhood town ?
Oh ! this way and that way—never stop.
'Tis picking up articles Grandma will drop;
'Tis kissing the baby's troubles away:
'Tis learning that cross words never will pay;
'Tis helping mother, 'tis sewing up rents;
'Tis reading and playing, 'tis saving cents;

'Tis loving and smiling, forgetting to frown:
Oh, that is the way to Womanhood town !

The Stars.

By LAURA F. ARMITAGE.

Our merry little Grace
  Had pressed her chubby face
Close to the window at the close of day;
  As fast as the stars came out,
  She gave a merry shout,
" Oh, see !" she said, " they're coming out to play."

" They are the fireflies,
  Far up there in the skies,
Who in the fields, last summer, used to play;
  But now cold weather's come,
  They all have gone back home.
I'm very glad I've found out where they stay."

The Robin.

(A recitation for Bird Day.)

Once there was a robin
  Lived outside the door,
Who wanted to go inside
  And hop upon the floor.
" Oh, no !" said the mother;
  " You must stay with me;
Little birds are safest
  Sitting in a tree."
" I don't care," said robin,

And gave his tail a fling;
" I don't think the old folks
    Know quite everything."
Down he flew, and kittie seized him
    Before he'd time to blink.
" Oh," he cried, " I'm sorry !
    But I didn't think."

A Queer Little Girl.

As queer a girl as ever was seen
Was little May Evelyn Caroline Green.
She sat a-wishing from morning till night
For everything in or out of her sight.

Her small brother Ned, who thought sister May
Was silly to spend her time wishing all day,
Told nurse in confidence, once after dinner,
That he was afraid she'd a wish-bone in her.

Thanksgiving.

(A recitation for a boy for Thanksgiving exercises.)

By JENNIE D. MOORE.

Pies of pumpkin, apple, mince,
Jams and jellies, peaches, quince,
Purple grapes and apples red,
Cakes and nuts and gingerbread—
    That's Thanksgiving.

Turkey ! Oh, a great big fellow !
Fruits, all ripe and rich and mellow;

Everything that's nice to eat,
More than I can now repeat—
    That's Thanksgiving.

Lots and lots of jolly fun,
Games to play and races run;
All as happy as can be
For 'tis happiness, you see,
    Makes Thanksgiving.

We must thank the One who gave
All the good things that we have.
That is *why* we keep the day
Set aside, our mammas say,
    For Thanksgiving.

Little Star.

Good-night, little star !
    I will go to my bed,
And leave you to burn
    While I lay down my head.

On my pillow I'll sleep
    Till the morning light;
Then you will be fading
    And I shall be bright.

The Flag of Freedom.
(A recitation for Flag Day.)

The flag of freedom here unfurled
    Is hailed by millions from afar—
The conquering standard of the world,
    Sublime alike in peace and war.

It proudly floats on every sea,
　Is honored now on every shore;
It whispers to the oppressed: " Be free,"
　And kindles hopes unknown before.

A Little Girl's Song of Autumn.

The autumn has filled me with wonder to-day,
The wind seems so sad, while the trees look so gay;
The sky is so blue, while the fields are so brown,
While bright leaves and brown leaves drift all
　　through the town.
　I wish I could tell why the world changes so;
　But I am a little girl—I cannot know !

The sun rises late, and then goes down so soon,
I think it is evening before it is noon !
Of the birds and the flowers hardly one can be
　found,
Though the little brown sparrows stay all the year
　round.
　I wish I could tell you where all the birds go;
　But I am a little girl—I cannot know !

O Autumn ! why banish such bright things as
　they ?
Pray turn the world gently ! don't scare them
　away !
And now they are gone, will you bring them
　again ?
If they come in the spring I may n't be here then.
　Why go they so swiftly, then come back so
　　slow ?
　Oh, I'm but a little girl—I cannot know.

A Lazy Boy's Idea.

By Rufus C. Langdon.

" Just drop a nickle in the slot ! "
  Well, now, that's very handy—
" Just drop a nickle in the slot ! "
  And, lo, you have your candy !

I know a boy who wishes that
  A slot, or perforation,
Were in his head through which he might
  Just drop an education.

There he could draw, from time to time,
  All kinds of information,
And never have to study more
  Against his inclination.

A foolish youth he is indeed,
  For not without a tussle
With schoolbooks can he hope to gain
  A wealth of mental muscle.

A shiftless boy is he as well—
  How wretched his condition !
Content to be a mere machine
  Without a grand ambition !

Harvest.

" You will reap what you sow," said the wise papa;
  And the wise little boy who heard
Said at once, " Then I'll plant some canary-seed,
  And perhaps I shall raise a bird."
                    —*Alice W. Rollins.*

My Bed Is A Boat.

(Recitation for a boy.)

My bed is like a little boat;
  Nurse helps me in when I embark;
She girds me in my sailor's coat
  And starts me in the dark.

At night I go on board, and say
  Good-night to all my friends on shore;
I shut my eyes and sail away,
  And see and hear no more.

And sometimes things to bed I take,
  As prudent sailors have to do :
Perhaps a slice of wedding-cake,
  Perhaps a toy or two.

All night across the dark we steer;
  But when the day returns at last,
Safe in my room, beside the pier,
  I find my vessel fast.
                    —*Robert Louis Stevenson.*

The Old Apple-Tree.

(A recitation for Arbor Day.)

I'm fond of the good apple-tree;
A very good-natured friend is he,
For, knock at his door whene'er you may,
He's always something to give away.

Shake him in winter : on all below
He'll send down a shower of feathery snow;
And when the spring sun is shining bright,
He'll fling down blossoms pink and white.

And when the summer comes so warm,
He shelters the little birds safe from harm;
And shake him in autumn, he will not fail
To send you down apples thick as hail.

Therefore it cannot a wonder be
That we sing Hurrah for the apple-tree !

The Bashful Marguerite.

Sweet Marguerite looked shyly from the grass
  Of country field, and softly whispered, " Here
I make my home, content; for I,—alas !—
  Am not the rose the city holds so dear ! "

Just then the Queen, driving by chance that way,
  Called to a page : " Bring me that Marguerite;
I am so tired of roses ! "—From that day
  The daisy had the whole world at her feet.
                                —*Alice W. Rollins.*

Every Little Helps.

What if a drop of rain should plead,
  " So small a drop as I
Can ne'er refresh the thirsty mead,
  I'll tarry in the sky."

What if the shining beam of noon,
    Should in its fountain stay,
Because its feeble light alone
    Cannot create a day ?

Does not each rain-drop help to form,
And every ray of light to warm
    And beautify, the flower ?

My Shadow.

I have a little shadow that goes in and out with me,
And what can be the use of him is more than I can
    see.
He is very, very like me from the heels up to the
    head;
And I see him jump before me, when I jump into
    my bed.

The funniest thing about him is the way he likes to
    grow—
Not at all like proper children, which is always
    very slow;
For he sometimes shoots up taller, like an india-
    rubber ball,
And he sometimes gets so little that there's none
    of him at all.

He hasn't got a notion of how children ought to
    play,
And can only make a fool of me in every sort of
    way.

He stays so close beside me, he's a coward, you can
    see;
I'd think shame to stick to nursie as that shadow
    sticks to me !

One morning, very early, before the sun was up,
I rose and found the shining dew on every butter-
    cup.
But my lazy little shadow, like an arrant sleepy-
    head,
Had stayed at home behind me and was fast asleep
    in bed.

             —*Robert Louis Stevenson.*

How the Week Goes.

By KATE WEST.

Monday rub, and Tuesday iron,
Wednesday lay the things away;
Thursday creep, and Friday sweep,
And Saturday bake for the Sabbath day.

Monday rub from tub to tub,
Monday rinse and twist and dry;
Tuesday shake and starch and smooth,
And hang the snow-white frills on high;

Wednesday pack them in the drawer;
Thursday scrub and shine the floor;
Friday with the pan and broom
Sweep the stairway, hall, and room;

Saturday we roast and bake
Cookies, pies, and golden cake,
Something, Sabbath day, to eat:
Thus the week is all complete.

He Didn't Think.

Once a trap was baited
  With a piece of cheese;
It tickled so a little mouse
  It almost made him sneeze.

An old rat said, " There's danger—
  Be careful where you go ! "
" Nonsense ! " said the other,
  " I don't think you know ! "

So he walked in boldly;
  Nobody in sight;
First he took a nibble,
  Then he took a bite.

Close the trap together
  Snapped as quick as wink,
Catching mousey fast there,
  'Cause he didn't think.
                 —*Phœbe Cary.*

What To Look For.

Do not look for wrong or evil,—
  You will find them if you do;
As you measure for your neighbor
  He will measure back to you.

Look for goodness, look for gladness,
  You will meet them all the while;
If you bring a smiling visage
  To the glass you meet a smile.
                 —*Alice Cary.*

How to Celebrate Arbor Day in the Schoolroom.

For the Primary, Grammar, and High School.

This book contains 96 solid pages. All the selections are fresh and new, and are selected both for their excellence and their practical usefulness in making up a program for the day. The following table of contents will give an idea of the book:

> I. THE ORIGIN OF ARBOR DAY.
> II. HINTS ON PLANTING THE TREES.
> III. ARBOR DAY IN THE U. S.
> IV. SPECIAL EXERCISES.

1. The Arbor Day Queen; 2. Thoughts About Trees; 3. Little Runaways; 4. November's Party; 5. The Coming of Spring; 6. Through the Year with the Trees; 7. May; 8. The Poetry of Spring; 9. The Plea of the Trees; 10. Tree Planting Exercise.

> V. RECITATIONS AND SONGS.
> VI. FIFTY QUOTATIONS.
> VII. THE PINK ROSE DRILL.
> VIII. ARBOR DAY PROGRAMS
> For Primary, Grammar, and High Schools.

Suggestions as to the most effective use of each exercise and recitation and the seven Arbor Day Programs are features which will be appreciated by the busy teacher.

Price, 25 Cents Postpaid.

How to Celebrate Washington's Birthday in the Schoolroom.

Containing Patriotic Exercises, Declamations, Recitations, Drills, Quotations, &c., for the
PRIMARY, GRAMMAR, AND HIGH SCHOOL.

96 Pages. Price, 25 Cents Postpaid.

This book has been received with great eagerness by teachers, and a large number sold. There are at least 100,000 teachers, who will hold some exercises on this great day. The observance of Washington's Birthday is increasing. It has recently been made compulsory in all the schools of New Jersey. No book is so good for preparing for it as this. The material is new and of a high order of merit. Here is a part of the

CONTENTS :

Special Exercises
His Birthday,
Tableaux and Recitations,
Our National Songs,
Historic Exercise,
Honoring the Flag,
Washington is Our Model,
Pictures from the Life of Washington,
Celebrating Washington's Birthday.

Recitations and Songs
The 22d of February,

I Would Tell.
Flag of the Rainbow,
The Good Old Days,
The School-House Stands by the Flag,
A Boy's Protest,
Tribute to Washington,
Our Presidents,
Flag of the Free.

Three Flag Drills

Fifty Patriotic Quotations.

Spring and Summer School Celebrations

EXERCISES, TABLEAUX, PANTOMIMES, RECITA-
TIONS, DRILLS, SONGS FOR CELEBRATING
EASTER, MAY DAY, MEMORIAL DAY,
FOURTH OF JULY, CLOSING DAY
IN THE SCHOOLROOM.

60 Pages. Price, 25 Cents Postpaid.

You have general exercises in your school, do you not? Then you need this book and should send for it now. It is illustrated. It contains nearly *one hundred* fresh, charming, mostly original selections.

PARTIAL TABLE OF CONTENTS:

Easter Song,	May and the Flowers,
Give Flowers to the Children,	The May Festival,
Easter in Early Days,	Gathering Flowers,
Sir Robin,	The Return of the Wanderers,
To the Flowers,	The Nation's Dead,
Wreath Drill and March,	In Memoriam,
Easter Time.	Zouave Drill,
Tableaux for Longfellow's King Robert	Program for Memorial Day,
of Sicily,	The Blue and the Gray,
A Bunch of Lilies.	The Nation's Birthday,
Greeting to May,	Stand by the Flag,
A Call to the Flowers,	Flag of Our Nation Great,
A Carpet of Green,	Boy's Marching Song,
To the Cuckoo,	The Poet's History of America,
To the Arbutus,	Etc., Etc.

Fancy Drills and Marches.

MOTION SONGS AND ACTION PIECES FOR ARBOR DAY,
CHRISTMAS DAY, MEMORIAL DAY, AND
PATRIOTIC OCCASIONS.

Price 25 Cents Postpaid.

THE LATEST, BRIGHTEST, AND BEST BOOK OF DRILLS.

Teachers who want something new and bright in the line of drills will certainly be greatly pleased with this book. One drill alone—Betz's Flag Grouping—has heretofore been sold for the price of this book, 25 cents.

PARTIAL TABLE OF CONTENTS:

Fancy Ribbon March. *Carl Betz.*	Wreath Drill and March.
Hatchet Drill for Feb. 22.	Rainbow Drill.
Christmas Tree Drill.	Glove Drill.
Wand Drill. *Mara L. Pratt.*	Tambourine Drill.
Delsarte Children. *M. D. Sterling.*	Flag Grouping and Posing. *Carl Betz.*
Zouave Drill.	Two Flag Drills.
Scarf Drill.	The March of the Red, White, and Blue.

Also many Motion Songs and Action Pieces. Full directions with each; fully illustrated,

The First Three Years of Childhood.

An exhaustive study of the psychology of children. By
BERNARD PEREZ. Edited and translated by Alice M.
Christie, translator of "Child and Child Nature," with
an introduction by James Sully, M. A., author of "Out-
lines of Psychology," etc. 12mo, cloth, 340 pp. Price,
$1.50; *to teachers*, $1.20; by mail, 10 cts. extra.

This is a comprehensive treatise on the psychology of childhood, and is a practical study of the human mind, not full
formed and equipped with knowledge, but as nearly as
possible, *ab origine*—before habit, environment, and education have asserted their sway and made their permanent
modifications. The writer looks into all the phases of child
activity. He treats exhaustively, and in bright Gallic style,
of sensations, instincts, sentiments, intellectual tendencies,
the will, the faculties of æsthetic and moral senses of young
children. He shows how ideas of truth and falsehood arise
in little minds, how natural is imitation and how deep is
credulity. He illustrates the development of imagination and
the elaboration of new concepts through judgment, abstraction, reasoning, and other mental methods. It is a book that
has been long wanted by all who are engaged in teaching,
and especially by all who have to do with the education and
training of children.

Our edition has a new index of special value and is beauti-
fully printed and elegantly and durably bound.

Prof. John Fiske, Harvard University: "It seems to me an excellent book and very much needed."

John Bascom, President University of Wisconsin: "A work of
marked interest to psychologists and intelligent parents."

B. A. Hinsdale, ex-Supt. Schools, Cleveland, Ohio: "I have exam-
ined the book with much pleasure and profit, and I sincerely hope you
may be successful in introducing it generally among the teachers of the
country."

Edwin C. Hewitt, President Illinois State Normal University:
"You have rendered an excellent service in bringing the book before
the public. I hope both your house and the public will profit by a
large sale."

**G. Stanley Hall, Professor of Psychology and Pedagogy, Johns
Hopkins University:** "I esteem the work a very valuable one for
primary and kindergarten teachers and for all interested in the psychology of childhood."

**Col. Francis W. Parker, Principal Cook County Normal and
Training School, Chicago:** "I am glad to see that you have published
Perez's wonderful work upon childhood. I shall do all I can to get
everybody to read it. It is a grand work."

Welch's Talks on Psychology Applied to

TEACHING. By A. S. WELCH, LL.D., Ex-Pres. of the Iowa Agricultural College at Ames, Iowa. Cloth, 16mo, 136 pp. Price, 50 cents; *to teachers*, 40 cents; by mail, 5 cents extra.

This little book has been written for the purpose of helping the teacher in doing more effective work in the school-room. The instructors in our schools are familiar with the branches they teach, but deficient in knowledge of the mental powers whose development they seek to promote. But no proficiency that does not include the *study of mind*, can ever qualify for the work of teaching. The teacher must comprehend fully not only the *objects* studied by the learner, but the *efforts* put forth and in studying them, the *effect* of these efforts on the faculty exerted, their *results* in the form of accurate knowledge. It is urged by eminent educators everywhere that a knowledge of the branches to be taught, and a *knowledge of the mind* to be trained thereby, are equally essential to successful teaching.

WHAT IT CONTAINS.

PART I.—Chapter 1. Mind Growth and its Helps. Chapter 2.—The Feelings. Chapter 3.—The Will and the Spontaneities. Chapter 4.—Sensation. Chapter 5.—Sense Perception, Gathering Concepts. Chapter 6.—Memory and Conception. Chapter 7.—Analysis and Abstraction. Chapter 8.—Imagination and Classification.—Chapter 9.—Judgment and Reasoning, the Thinking Faculties.

PART II.—Helps to Mind Growth. Chapter 1.—Education and the Means of Attaining it. Chapter 2 —Training of the Senses. Chapter 3 —Reading, Writing, and Spelling. Chapter 4.—Composition, Elementary Grammar, Abstract Arithmetic, etc.

*** This book, as will be seen from the contents, deals with the subject differently from Dr. Jerome Allen's " Mind Studies for Young Teachers," (same price) recently published by us.

FROM THOSE WHO HAVE SEEN IT.

Co. Insp. Dearness, London, Canada.--"Here find it the most lucid and practical introduction to mental science I have ever seen."

Florida School Journal.—" Is certainly the best adapted and most desirable for the mass of teachers."

Penn. School Journal.—"Earnest teachers will appreciate it."

Danville, Ind., Teacher and Examiner.—" We feel certain this book has a mission among the primary teachers."

Iowa Normal Monthly.—" The best for the average teacher."

Prof. H. H. Seeley, Iowa State Normal School.—"I feel that you have done a very excellent thing for the teachers. Am inclined to think we will use it in some of our classes."

Science, N. Y.—"Has been written from an educational point of view."

Education, Boston.—" Aims to help the teacher in the work of the school-room."

Progressive Teacher.—"There is no better work."

Ev-Gov. Dysart, Iowa.—" My first thought was, ' What a pity it could not be in the hands of every teacher in Iowa."

www.ingramcontent.com/pod-product-compliance
Lightning Source LLC
Chambersburg PA
CBHW030002030726
47499CB00008B/2853